Not Like That!

For JJ, my inspiration for this book! LJ

First published in 2010
by Wayland

Text copyright © Louise John
Illustration copyright © Catalina Alvarez

Wayland
338 Euston Road
London NW1 3BH

Wayland Australia
Level 17/207 Kent Street
Sydney, NSW 2000

Series Editor: Louise John
Editor: Katie Powell
Cover design: Paul Cherrill
Design: D.R.ink
Consultant: Shirley Bickler

A CIP catalogue record for this book is available from the British Library.

ISBN 9781526302335

Printed in China

Wayland is a division of Hachette Children's Books,
an Hachette UK Company

www.hachette.co.uk

Not Like That!

Written by Louise John
Illustrated by Catalina Alvarez

WAYLAND

"Let's put the tent up," said Mum.

"I can put the tent up," said Dad. "Get me the poles, please."

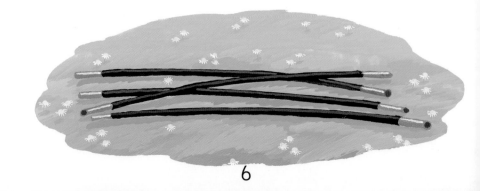

Dad put the poles in.

"Not like that, Dad!"
said Olly.

"I can do it," said Dad.
"Get me the pegs, please."

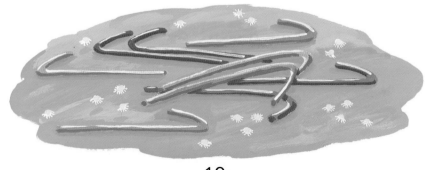

Dad put the pegs in.

"Not like that, Dad!"
said Cara.

13

"I can put up a tent!" said Dad. "Get me the ropes, please."

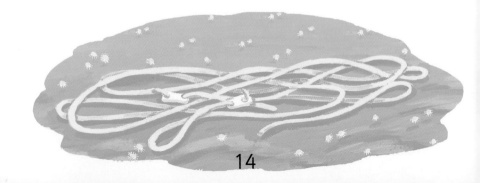

"Not like that, Dad!"
said Olly.

"Oh, dear!" said Mum.
"Let me help."

"I can do it," said Dad.
"Look! The tent is up!"

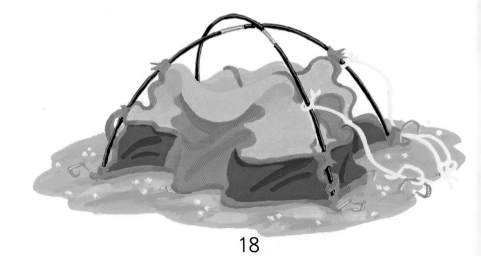

Crash!

"Oh, dear!" said Mum.
"Let's put the tent
up again!"

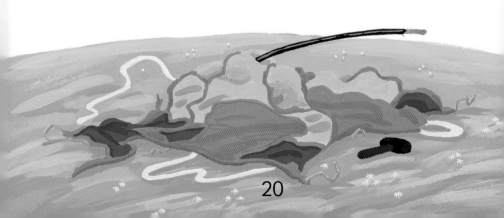

Guiding a First Read of
Not Like That!

It is important to talk through the book with your child before they read it alone. This prepares them for the way the story unfolds, and allows them to enjoy the pictures as you both talk naturally, using the language they will later encounter when reading. Read them the brief overview, and then follow the suggestions below:

1. Talking through the book

The family were going camping and Dad was sure he knew how to put up the tent. First, Olly and then Cara and then Mum tried to help him, but he just wouldn't listen!

Let's read the title: Not Like That!
On page 4, the family were at the camping ground and Mum said, "Let's put the tent up." Now turn the page. Dad wanted to do it. He asked Olly for the poles.
But on page 8, was Olly happy with the way Dad was doing it?

Continue through the book, guiding the discussion to fit the text as your child looks at the illustrations.

On page 18, Dad thought he'd got the tent up. Was he right? Turn to page 20. Crash! Oh dear! They had to put it up again!

2. A first reading of the book

Ask your child to read the book independently, pointing carefully underneath each word (tracking), while thinking about the story. Praise attempts by your child to correct themselves, and prompt them to use their letter knowledge, the punctuation, and check the meaning, for example:

On page 6, Dad could have asked for 'posts'. The word starts with 'p'. But can you see the 'l' in the middle? The word says 'poles'.

Well done. You sounded out 'p-e-g-s', and then you read the whole sentence and checked the picture.

3. Follow-up activities

The high frequency words in this title are:
can   do   get   I   in   it   like   me   not   put   said   that   the   up

- Select two high frequency words, and ask your child to find them throughout the book. Discuss the shape of the letters and their letter sounds.
- To memorise the words, ask your child to write them in the air, then write them repeatedly on a whiteboard or on paper, leaving a space between each attempt.

4. Encourage

- Reading the book again – with expression.
- Drawing a picture based on the story.
- Writing one or two sentences using the practised words.

23

START READING is a series of highly enjoyable books for beginner readers. **The books have been carefully graded to match the Book Bands widely used in schools.** This enables readers to be sure they choose books that match their own reading ability.

Look out for the Band colour on the book in our Start Reading logo.

The Bands are:

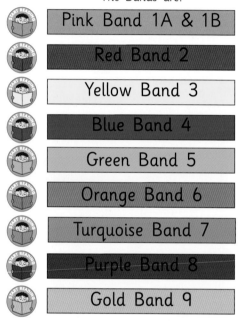

Pink Band 1A & 1B

Red Band 2

Yellow Band 3

Blue Band 4

Green Band 5

Orange Band 6

Turquoise Band 7

Purple Band 8

Gold Band 9

START READING books can be read independently or shared with an adult. They promote the enjoyment of reading through satisfying stories supported by fun illustrations.

Louise John is really the editor of Start Reading, but wanted to see how she liked writing books, too. It was quite tricky, but she found that eating lots of chocolate biscuits made her think better! She tries out her ideas on her daughter, Amelia, who tells her if they are any good or not!

Catalina Alvarez lives in Sherwood, Nottingham with her son Oscar and two cats called Lizzie and Winnie. She has illustrated more books than she can count, especially lots of phonics books. Her favourite one is called 'Pog the Dog!'